CHI

6/07

FRIENDS
OF ACPL

P9-AQZ-015

A Note to Parents

Read to your child...

★ Reading aloud is one of the best ways to develop your child's love of reading. Read together at least 20 minutes each day.

★ Laughter is contagious! Read with feeling. Show your child that reading is fun.

★ Take time to answer questions your child may have about the story. Linger over pages that interest your child.

...and your child will read to you.

★ Do not correct every word your child misreads. Instead, say, "Does that make sense? Let's try it again."

★ Praise your child as he progresses. Your encouraging words will build his confidence.

You can help your Level 2 reader.

★ Keep the reading experience interactive. Read part of a sentence, then ask your child to add the missing word.

★ Read the first part of a story. Then ask, "What's going to happen next?"

★ Give clues to new words. Say, "This word begins with *b* and ends in *ake*, like *rake, take, lake*."

★ Ask your child to retell the story using her own words.

★ Use the five *W*s: WHO is the story about? WHAT happens? WHERE and WHEN does the story take place? WHY does it turn out the way it does?

Most of all, enjoy your reading time together!

—**Bernice Cullinan, Ph.D.,**
Professor of Reading, New York University

Published by Reader's Digest Children's Books
Reader's Digest Road, Pleasantville, NY U.S.A. 10570-7000 and
Reader's Digest Children's Publishing Limited,
The Ice House, 124-126 Walcot Street, Bath UK BA1 5BG
Copyright © 2000 Reader's Digest Children's Publishing, Inc.
All rights reserved. Reader's Digest Children's Books is a trademark and
Reader's Digest and All-Star Readers are registered trademarks of
The Reader's Digest Association, Inc. Fisher-Price trademarks are used
under license from Fisher-Price, Inc., a subsidiary of
Mattel, Inc., East Aurora, NY 14052 U.S.A.
©2000 Mattel, Inc. All Rights Reserved.
Printed in Hong Kong.
10 9 8 7 6

Library of Congress Cataloging-in-Publication Data

Mann, Paul Z.
    I can jump higher / by Paul Z. Mann ; illustrated by Chris Demarest.
      p. cm.—(All-star readers. Level 2)
    Summary: A boy named Sam and a girl named Claire boast to one another
  about all the outrageous physical feats they can perform.
    ISBN 1-57584-658-6 (pbk. : alk. Paper)
    [1. Play—Fiction. 2. Friendship—Fiction. 3. Stories in rhyme.]
  I. Demarest, Chris L., ill. II. Title. III. Series.
PZ8.3.M35535Iaan   2000   [E]—dc21   00-028610

I Can Jump Higher!

by Paul Z. Mann
illustrated by Chris Demarest

All-Star Readers®

Reader's Digest Children's Books™
Pleasantville, New York • Montréal, Québec

Allen County Public Library

The day was dull.
The sky was gray.
Claire said to Sam,
"What can we play?"

"Let's swing," said Sam.
Claire said, "That's dumb."
Sam frowned. Claire frowned.
She smacked her gum.

"Look! I can blow
a bubble, Sam!
Look! Are you looking?"

"Yes, I am."

Claire blew and blew.

"Not bad at all,"
said Sam. "But still,
it's pretty small."

"I can blow a big one, Claire.
So big it lifts me in the air.
Up and up into the sky—"
"Go on," said Claire.
"Go on and try."

"Not now," said Sam.
Claire asked, "How come?"
Sam shrugged. "I'm out
of bubble gum."

"I know!" said Sam.
"Let's climb that tree."
Claire frowned. "That tree's
too small for me."

3 1833 05216 2093

"Me, too," said Sam.
"That tree's too small.
I climb up trees
ten times that tall!"

"Me, too," said Claire.
"I love to climb.
Up, up, up, up
all the time.

I climbed a tree
so high," said Claire,
"the clouds were getting
in my hair."

"I jumped up to
the clouds one time,"
said Sam. "It takes
too long to climb."

"You jumped?" said Claire.
"That's very high."
Sam said, "It only
took one try."

"Not bad," said Claire.
"But yesterday,
I jumped up to the moon."
"*No way!*"

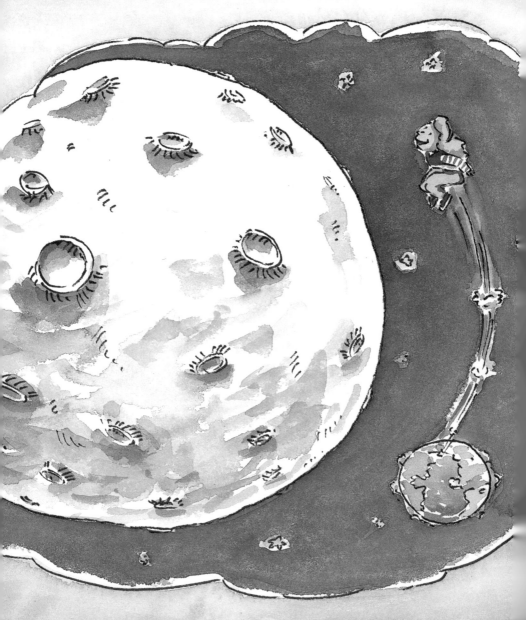

Claire smiled. "I did.
I'll show you how."
"Okay…"
"But not," said Claire, "right now."

"Let's race!" said Sam.
"I'll win, of course,"
said Claire. "Last week
I beat a horse."

"That's fast.
But I will win, I bet,"
said Sam. "Last week
I beat a jet!"

"Did not!"   "Did, too!"

"Did not!"   "Did, too!
                    It wasn't even
                    hard to do!"

"Or we can swim,"
Sam said. "That's fun.
I swim much faster
than I run.

I swim much faster
than the fish.
I'll show you how—"
Claire smiled. "You wish!"

"I swim," said Claire.
"I swim fast, too.
I swim much faster
than you do.

I'm faster than
a ship with sails.
I'm faster than
the fastest whales!"

"I know! Let's wrestle,
Sam," said Claire.
"I've wrestled with
a polar bear!"

Sam said, "*I* beat an alligator!"
"*When?*"
Sam smiled. "I'll tell you later."

The sun was low.
The day was through.
They still did not know
what to do.
They sat and no one
said a thing.

At last, Claire said,
"I know! Let's swing!"
"Let's swing!" said Sam.
"That's lots of fun.
Let's go! The day
is almost done."

"Look, Claire! We've almost reached the moon!"

"Keep swinging, Sam!
We'll be there soon!"

Words are fun!

Here are some simple activities you can do with a pencil, crayons, and a sheet of paper. You'll find the answers at the bottom of the page.

───── ★ ─────

1. Match the words that rhyme—even though they may not be spelled the same way.

hair	blew
jet	bear
through	done
fun	bet
sails	whales

2. Match the words that are opposites:

high	tall
frown	slow
short	small
fast	low
big	smile

3. Draw a picture of yourself floating away on a cloud to a very special place. Where would you like to go?

4. Find the word in each group that is NOT an action word.

swim	shoe	eat
berry	play	wrestle
run	cloud	kick
fly	float	sky
climb	paper	sing
sweet	jump	throw

ANSWERS:
1. hair=bear; jet=bet; through=blew; fun=done; sails=whales
2. high/low; frown/smile; short/tall; fast/slow; big/small
4. shoe; berry; cloud; sky; paper; sweet